A Nation Divided: Journeys of Mahesh and Annmarie

By Mikhail Nair Lobo and Raphael Nair Lobo

Printed in India

IndiePress

ISBN: 978-93-6045-884-3

First Printing, 2024

IndiePress

A division of Nasadiya Technologies Private Ltd.

Koramangala, Bangalore

Karnataka-560029

http://indiepress.in/

Edited by Anagha Somanakoppa

Typeset by Pratik Bhamare

Art Direction and Cover Design by Ananya

Illustrations by Pratilipi Comics

Publishing Consultant – Zoheb Ahmed

Preface

Mikhail and Raphael are twins living in Mumbai. They're both very creative kids who love art, music and writing along with the usual Minecraft, Roblox and (in my opinion, nonsensical) YouTube shots.

When they were 11, they were taken on a school trip to Amritsar where they visited The Partition Museum among other sites. They talked at length about everything they saw and did in Amritsar including the Golden Temple, the Attari border but only mentioned The Partition Museum in passing. I thought perhaps they were too young to understand the gravitas of the partition and the many hardships people went through. It was only when they wrote these stories that I realised what a deep impact the visit had on them.

I'm grateful to the wonderful people at The Partition Museum who have kept these stories alive and thus have enabled newer generations to empathise with the victims of the partition. A big thank you also to Ascend International School for taking students to Amritsar and then encouraging them to write.

It took me 2 years to finally get this published- I'm so grateful to my father, Raj Nair who pushed me to get it done.

And finally thank you Miki and Rafa for being the sensitive, empathetic and creative boys that you are. Daddy and I could never have imagined the two brats who kept us awake all night would one day be writing stories.

- Gayatri Nair Lobo

Contents

Story 1

Fractured Lands and Whole Hearts

BY MIKHAIL NAIR LOBO

Introduction

The sun rose across the horizon, painting the dawning sky with vibrant hues of orange, purple, and red. Our room was small, and my family shared one bed. As my parents slept, I drew the curtains and gazed through the circular window. The city of Bombay slowly came into view. I pressed my face closer to the glass, watching as the saturated blue ocean split against the bow of the boat. I pulled back and gently shook my parents awake. I watched them lift their heads from the pillow, still groggy. "We're here," I whispered, glancing back at the window.

My father quickly got out of bed and headed towards the small restroom on the boat. I heard the metal of his badge clink as he put on his uniform. I helped my mother make the bed, folding the blankets and tucking them under the bedsheets. I placed the pillows neatly and took a few steps back, feeling proud of my work. This routine had become second nature during our two-and-a-half-month boat journey to our destination. I flipped through the dresses in my cupboard and picked out my favourite one, which I had been saving for our arrival. The dress, made from the softest and finest lamb's wool, felt comforting as I spread my hands across it. I slipped into the dress and twirled around, watching it spin with me.

My mother finished getting ready, and we were set to go. "We will have a wonderful time in India, won't we, Anne?" My father asked as he tied his shoelaces. I nodded. My name is Annmarie Edwards, and I am the daughter of George and Agatha Edwards. I am eleven years old, soon to be twelve. My father is in the British Army, and we moved to India because of his military assignment. My mother was initially hesitant about the move, but she decided to come with him. The army allowed us to live in India, and here we are. I had read books about India and marvelled at its beauty. I love reading and writing; it's what I do in my spare time. As thoughts of living in India swirled through my mind, I blinked, grounding myself. A horn blew as the ship docked. My father slid the door open, and we stepped out. As I walked down the aisle, my head filled with thoughts, almost overwhelming me, until I took a deep breath, inhaling the distinct scent of India's air.

Chapter 1

Is this... Home?

An aroma of dead fish filled the air. I gagged and plugged my nostrils. This wasn't the best first impression of the country I'd be living in. My mother grabbed my hand and pulled me towards a queue. Her grip was always tight when she felt nervous. I stood in line, trying to peek outside the exit. My mother held me close, her arms wrapped around mine. My eyes scanned the area outside, catching a glimpse of my father. "Father?" I looked at the exit, then back at my mother.

"Darling, he's doing another march, just as before we boarded the boat," she explained. The army has fascinated me since I was young. We used to go to parades and watch the soldiers march back and forth along a narrow path between crowds of people. My father was recently recruited into the army, and I was more than excited. I shook free from my mother's grip, eager for a closer look. "Annie, not now," she told me patiently.

I heard trumpets, drums, and the clanking of leather boots on the ground, accompanied by the general shouting commands. After a few minutes, the sounds faded, replaced by a grand applause. I joined in and clapped. The queue moved forward, little by little. As soon as we exited, the sun shone brightly, and a hot ray of sunlight beat down on the docks. My father joined the rest of the army, and my mother followed the other passengers, pulling me along even though I longed to be with my father.

We stayed in a small room, only slightly larger than the one on the ship. The navy had arranged these rooms for recruits moving to India. However, we didn't plan to stay there today. My father wanted to take us to Rajasthan, Gujarat, and other parts of India. Our luggage remained unpacked, and we slept in the same clothes. The sunlight was intense, making it feel as though Earth had drifted closer to the sun. My mother handed me a foldable fan she had brought from England. I opened it and fanned myself.

We boarded the ship, and I was amazed by its size. I examined the seats, railings, and the boat's interior. The boat rocked occasionally, causing me to lose my balance. The flooring was made of slippery, polished wood. Mom held my hand tightly as we searched for a seat. She told me to sit next to the railing. I looked over and watched the water splash around. My parents went to greet the captain. Before leaving, my mother reminded me not to bend over the railing. I waited for them to leave and then ignored her warning. I held the railing, noticing the rusting metal. A horn blew, and the boat started moving forward. I watched the waves created by the boat's movement.

After a while, I looked up; the city was no longer in sight. We were in the middle of the ocean. I looked back, searching for my parents, but they were nowhere to be seen. I leaned over the railing, trying to spot a fish or two. Being on the top floor, I couldn't see any. I leaned even further for a closer look. Suddenly, the boat rocked, and I lost my balance. My stomach slipped over the railing, and I plunged into the ocean. "MUM!" I screamed, but no one heard me. The water hit me hard, sending pain all over my body. I tried to push the water away and lift myself, but it was no use. Saltwater stung my eyes and filled my mouth as I screamed. My hair floated thickly around me as my body started to sink. I reached out, but I continued to sink deeper. Still conscious, I struggled to float back to the surface. I let out another scream underwater, but only bubbles escaped, and my voice was muffled. I felt a thunk on my head, and pain surged through me. Then everything went black, all within less than a minute.

Chapter 2

I Wish I Were Dead

I wish I had died when I fell off the boat. But here I am. My eyelids slowly opened. I felt my skin against a rough yet soft surface. As I opened my eyes, I watched waves crash onto a beach. I was lying on the sand under the hot sun. Using my arms, I pushed myself up, but a sensation in my throat made me cough up seawater. After clearing my throat, I stood up and noticed a bruise all over my shin. Sand had gotten into the bruise, causing a stinging sensation. I figured someone had saved me and brought me to this shore, but I had no idea who. Looking around, I saw a city in the distance and started limping towards it. Boats and fishing nets surrounded me, and the smell of dead fish filled the air. With a glimmer of hope, I made my way towards the city.

The hot afternoon sun burned down on me as I limped across the roads. I kept my gaze down, but I could feel eyes on me. It's not every day you see a British eleven-year-old walking down the street, unaccompanied and covered in sand. It hadn't fully hit me yet. I felt numb, devoid of emotion. Finding shade between two short buildings, I sat down and curled up into a ball. It was only then that I realised the gravity of my situation. I was away from my parents in a country I knew nothing about. I lay there, trembling, and soon, a sob escaped me, followed by a flood of tears. I spent the rest of the afternoon crying, unable to stop. It wasn't just the fear of being lost; it was the crushing loneliness. My face felt raw from the tears, and I whimpered in the alley. What do I do now?

As I lay on the cobbled ground, the pain in my injured leg flared up again. I clutched my leg, trying to alleviate the pain, and cried even louder. Across the street, I spotted a stray puppy attempting to cross the road. Its eyes appeared to lack pupils, and I realised it was blind. Ignoring the pain, I lifted myself up and hopped towards the puppy, holding out my arm for it to sniff. It seemed frightened at first but then calmed down. I gently stroked the fur between its ears. After a while, I picked up the puppy and carried it back to the alley. My tears seemed to recede, replaced by occasional sniffles. "Good girl, good girl," I whispered, my voice breaking from pain and sorrow. The puppy fell asleep in my arms, and the shade cooled its fur. We both began to yawn and soon fell asleep, our heartbeats in sync.

As we slept, I thought about blind people and Helen Keller, the woman who popularised Braille. The puppy's fur felt comforting in my arms, making me feel loved. I decided to name her Keller.

Chapter 3

Keller

I lay on the ground, feeling suddenly ill. My vision blurred, and it felt as if the world had lost its orbit and was spinning endlessly. My head throbbed, and I clutched it in pain. I heard Keller whimper beside me, her fur brushing against me just before everything went black. It felt as if my eyeballs had rolled back, and my pupils were facing inward. I cried out, "Keller, help!" But my strength faded, and I could no longer hold myself up. I closed my eyes, and my body collapsed, my head hitting the cobblestones of the alley. This time, the world stayed black.

When I opened my eyes again, my mouth felt wet. Keller was sitting next to me, whimpering, unaware that I was awake. I tapped the concrete softly, and I saw a surge of excitement in her. She trotted over and licked my face. I scratched her fur, and she lay down beside me. Looking around, I noticed water remnants and a bamboo bucket where Keller had been sitting. It dawned on me that she had brought the water. I hugged Keller tightly, petting her vigorously as she panted with excitement, jumping around me. I giggled, realising that Keller had saved my life.

As I scratched under her neck, I felt a patch of matted fur and discovered a collar. It dawned on me that Keller was a military dog, trained to save lives, and had reacted quickly when I fainted. I wondered how she had gone blind, but the thought was too painful to dwell on. Instead, I held Keller close, petting her as she comforted me. At that moment, it felt like it was just us in the world—me and Keller. And that, I thought, was worth more than anything.

Chapter 4

Life

Being independent does not mean being apart.

This morning, I woke up with a start, hearing shouting and screaming. I jumped to my feet and ran across the street, holding Keller in my arms. Parades filled the city, and flags were being hoisted. The British flag had changed; it was now orange, green, and white with a blue circle in the middle. I strained to listen to the chanting. "India! India! India!" It dawned on me what was happening—India was free from my country. A sense of rage bubbled up inside me but then, conflicting thoughts flashed through my mind. Was I supposed to be angry? I watched as faces lit up with joy, each person celebrating. I didn't know what to feel anymore. Keller whimpered, scared by the loud noises. As I observed the celebration, a few Indians noticed me. My heart raced, and I felt it in my throat. I turned around, and Keller started barking. What began as a walk turned into a sprint, and I ran. Footsteps followed, and Keller whimpered and barked. I started crying. Yells echoed behind me as I ran. I stopped to catch my breath, panting heavily. Looking back, I saw a crowd of men and women running. One of them held a small gun, like a pistol, and I screamed at the top of my lungs. I put Keller down and held out my arms, sniffling and sobbing. I heard the gun being loaded as people around me screamed. I burst into tears, and within seconds, I heard a gunshot. Pain shot through my arm, and I realised I was caught in the crossfire. Keller howled as the bullet grazed my arm. It didn't go through, but it hurt. I collapsed, passing out. The world went black for the third time on my trip to India. Was this a sign that I wasn't meant to be here?

I thought I would never wake up, never see the sun again, and that I had blacked out for the last time. But as I woke up, I saw Keller by my side once more. Her fur was splattered with blood. I looked at my arm, wincing as I raised my head. Keller had torn my dress apart, leaving me in just leggings and a shirt, using the dress as a bandage to wrap around my arm. The sky was dark, and we were lying in the same spot where I had been shot. The pain was unbearable, and I struggled to endure it. "Thank you, Keller," I tried to say. Keller had saved me twice before despite being blind. She jumped up in excitement, which I took as a thank you for when I saved her life while she was crossing the street. But I owed her much more than that. As days and nights passed, my wound began to heal, although slowly. The bullet had been sharp but hadn't caused too much damage. I was fortunate that it hadn't cut too deeply. The pain lessened over time, though it still hurt. I started counting the days, trying to keep track, but couldn't maintain the habit. As nights and days went by, a full moon rose in the sky. As I lay there under the moonlight, a crumpled piece of paper blew towards me. I grabbed it and realised it was a newspaper. My eyes scanned the paper, looking for my father's name, remembering that I was still searching for him. My eyes drifted to the headline:

"Partition begins along religious lines." I kept re-reading the article, unable to comprehend the idea of splitting India. The bold black letters jumbled in my mind as I tried to imagine India being torn apart. The thoughts gave me a headache. What would happen? Why was this happening because of religion? Was this good? Keller whimpered again as if sensing my turmoil. I gently rubbed her, and she quieted down, falling asleep. But I couldn't sleep. My mind was a storm of thoughts, causing another headache.

Chapter 5

Partition

Before I knew it, the streets started to get crowded. Keller and I moved to another alley, smaller and darker than the previous one. I was scared of being spotted and wanted to remain hidden. The new alley was dark and deep, which wasn't comforting, but it was our only choice. Every day, I saw people walking across the street with bags on their backs and heads, looking exhausted and defeated. Their faces were drawn, and their backs were hunched. Many were coming and going from this town, likely due to the partition. People had to move to different countries based on their religion.

Among the crowd, I noticed a girl walking with her parents. She looked younger than me, and I felt a strong urge to meet her. Aside from Keller, I had no other friends. I started limping towards her, using parts of my dress to cover my bullet wounds, hoping she wouldn't notice. I kept my head down, fearing another attack. Suddenly, I heard an explosion, followed by a scream. Everyone froze in their tracks. As I looked up, gasps and screams filled the air. A man had collapsed in the middle of the crowd. Horrified, I screamed. Then I heard the sound of a gun being loaded, and I froze, flashbacks of my previous injury playing in my mind. Another bullet flew past me, hitting an old woman. I cried, glancing at the girl. Tears welled up in her eyes. She looked left and right, and our eyes met.

She didn't break her stare. I could read her eyes like a book... **Help.**

Her mother screamed and let go of her hand, running away. Her father tried to pull her along, but she didn't move, so he ran off alone. I cried and sprinted towards her. She burst into tears as her parents disappeared from sight. "Ma!" she screamed repeatedly. "Papa!" We stood there, staring at each other. Despite the danger surrounding us, it felt like everything had gone silent. "M-Ma," she croaked as if that were all she could say. I grabbed her hand tightly, and she looked at me with fear. I tried to reassure her, saying, "I'm not here with bad intentions; I'm here to help." She may not have understood my words, but she seemed to trust me. I pulled her towards the alley, her loud cries echoing in the background. As we ran, I thought about my decision to help a girl I had just met. It felt like the right choice. Even if I never find my parents, I'll strive to find peace in this world.

Chapter 6

Saira

As we ran, with destruction and death behind us, the girl cried. India was no longer a country but a dangerous zone. We squeezed through the narrow entrance of an alley, and as soon as we arrived, the girl collapsed in tears. I sat next to her, my own eyes brimming with tears. Keller howled continuously, and I scratched her between her ears to comfort her. Eventually, we fell silent, and the girl managed a soft smile. She spoke a few words in her language, trying to hold back tears. I smiled, even though I didn't understand. "My name is Annmarie," I told her, pointing to myself. She giggled slightly and repeated my name. She pointed to herself and said, "Saira." I repeated her name, and she had to correct me a few times. We smiled at each other, momentarily forgetting the chaos outside. Keller sat beside me. "Keller, we have a friend here," I whispered, looking at Saira. Although she may not have understood my words, she played with Keller. I tried to explain that Keller was blind, and Saira frowned in realisation. "Do you know English?" I asked. She didn't respond; she just looked at me, so I realised she didn't understand. Keller licked my face, and I stroked her fur. Keller lay in my arms and fell asleep, with Saira petting her. As we lay in the alley, where sunlight couldn't reach, I thought of my parents. What were they doing? Had they forgotten about me?

Before I knew it, time had sped by. Saira and I never spoke, yet we felt a connection, like telepathy, passing through our minds. I could sense when Saira was sad, and when I did, I squeezed her hand in mine. Every day, I went to the beach and strolled through the fish market stalls. One specific stall sold cooked fish, and I would watch as the vendor cooked the fish until it turned a crispy orange color outside. Despite the unpleasant smell at the market, I starved day after day and couldn't bear not looking at food. Every few days, I would steal a couple of fish from the storage compartment in the stall, sneaking them back to the alley, and nibbling on them sparingly. I wrapped them in the newspaper I had found on the road.

Today, my stomach roared, and I felt sick. It was never full, always slightly hollow. I tapped Saira on her shoulder and smiled. She gave me a fake smile in return and helped herself up. I held her hand, and we slipped through the tight entrance of the alley. Keller raised her head and followed. She often banged her head on the walls, but she made it through this time. Saira sniffed the air and smiled. I giggled, wondering how she could like the smell. The fish market was full of fish in different sizes and shapes, and Saira watched in awe. I kept my head down while walking through the market. I pulled Saira between two stalls where there was a boulder. She looked confused, but I pulled her behind it. I peeped out and saw the stall and smoke rising into the sky. The vendor flipped a fish into a pan with a utensil and walked over to a different stall. The fish smelled delicious, and my stomach grumbled again. I pictured my usual procedure in my mind. The plan was ready.

Chapter 7

The Plan

Keller howled as I sneaked towards the mouth-watering stall. I motioned to Saira to quiet Keller down. Saira wrapped Keller in her arms, snuggling with her. The evening sun dipped into its golden hour, casting a warm glow across the horizon. Vendors called out, promoting their stalls, and the stench of raw fish wafted through the air. In front of me lay the fried fish. I could almost taste the crispness and the crunch as we would bite into it. I reached for a bag in another compartment and slipped the fish inside. Although there were people around, no one noticed me. I felt invisible, in a good way—I didn't want to be noticed. I raced back to Saira and Keller, with Keller pouncing at the smell of the fish. As we walked back to the alley, I slipped a slightly cooked fish from another stall. We ran back to the alley, grinning from ear to ear.

I had become accustomed to the bullet wound, so I didn't flinch while moving. I placed the hot fish on the pale concrete bricks, using the bag as a napkin, and nibbled on it little by little. The first bite was heavenly, with flavours bursting on my tongue and spices galore. Though I stole the same two fish every day, this time felt different. Saira let out a satisfied gasp as she took a bite. I gave Keller the other fish, carefully removing the bones. I knew she couldn't handle the spices, so I always got her a slightly cooked fish with no added spices. She gobbled it up before I could even hand it to her. Saira and I laughed until the sun began to set. We lay in the alley, hoping for a better tomorrow. Over the next few days, Saira and I became best friends, but today, we didn't go out to get fish.

This morning, Saira stepped outside for a stroll on the beach. I followed, with Keller tagging along. The beach was beautiful, with bright blue water and beige sand. As we sat on the sand, watching the sunrise, I heard someone shout. Saira seemed to snap back to reality, her mood shifting from happiness to worry. I realised she understood what the man had said. I gave her a puzzled look, and she tried to explain. "Chug. Choo. Choo?" she said nervously. I shook my head in confusion. "Pakistan!" she cried out, bursting into tears. She lowered her head, covering her eyes with her palms. The word sounded familiar. I remembered the newspaper I had seen—India was split and partitioned. I realised the other half was Pakistan. Saira was leaving India to go to Pakistan. I signalled that I understood. She looked at me with eyes full of tears. I will save her and take her home.

Chapter 8

Pakistan

The train station was packed, even though many people had left last week. I managed to find my way there, and Saira was very thankful for my help. Keller was in my arms as we stood at the station, surrounded by a crowd so dense that there was barely any room to breathe. The air was filled with the stench of sweat. We found a spot to stand next to each other. Suddenly, I heard a howl and motioned for Keller to be quiet, but it wasn't Keller. A train screeched as it braked in front of the station. The crowd rushed to get on, and before even a quarter of the people could board, the train was full. People climbed onto the roof of the train, trying to find space. It was disheartening to see how little room there was, knowing we might not fit. I looked at Saira, and she looked back. Feeling the crowd push from behind, I grabbed Saira's hand, and we climbed up to the roof, with Keller barking in my other hand. We found a spot on top, not too close to the edge but not too crowded either. Before we knew it, the train started moving, whistling as it ran along the rails. I looked back at the station, hearing the cries of those left behind. I felt bad for them, knowing they might never make it home and could be attacked. As the hot sun rose over the horizon, our journey began. I didn't care how long it took; I was determined to bring happiness to Saira, no matter what.

Many days and nights passed, and Saira and I stayed and slept on top of the train, even though it was dangerous. The scenery was beautiful, but by midday, the sun had baked us alive. The hills were majestic, hanging high above the railway. Soon enough, the train crossed the border, and we reached Pakistan. The place was beautiful as soon as we got off the train. Thankfully, I was greeted with a pleasant scent, not the stench of fish. The night sky blanketed Pakistan, and I held Saira's hand as we walked through the railway station. The lights on the station roofs flickered. I noticed that Saira's nervous expression had softened slightly. After strolling through the station for a while, Saira yawned. I loosened my grip and sat down on the cobbled road. Saira copied me, resting her head on her knees. I heard her whimper and pat her shoulder. She looked up with tears in her eyes. I gave her a soft smile. "Don't worry, Saira," I told her, even though she might not understand. Maybe it was the tone I used, but she seemed comforted. Nearby, I heard crying from a bench. A couple sat there, a dress draped over them like a blanket, sobbing non-stop. I felt bad. Had they lost someone like me and Saira? As I looked at them, so did Saira. Suddenly, she jumped to her feet and screamed,

"Mama! Papa!"

Chapter 9

What Even is Hope?

"Saira?" a lady called from the bench. Saira ran towards them, tears streaming down her face. I watched as they hugged each other for what felt like a few minutes. I smiled, feeling happy for her, but when Saira pointed at me and her parents smiled from afar, jealousy filled me. Why her and not me? I felt angry, wanting us both to have the same happy ending. Why should she get one, especially after I have saved her? Saira and her parents looked at me, confused, perhaps wondering how to help me. I saw them walk away, looking back at me. I think they were trying to get someone who could speak to me in English. I sat there, Keller asleep in my arms, wishing she would always stay a puppy—so easy to cuddle. I sulked with her as the early morning sun began to rise. The train station soon emptied, and I started to lose hope. I had travelled to another country once again, this time with no hope. The alley had felt like home to me. It may not have been like my home back in Great Britain, with its furniture, bed, and more, but it provided shelter, and that was all that mattered. Now, I was sitting in an empty train station, waiting for Saira, in a country I'd never been to before, with a blind dog in my arms. I couldn't stop crying, and my face felt numb. I looked around; no one was there. Keller whimpered in her sleep, and I calmed her down. We felt the same way.

I heard a car driving by the road on the other side of the train station. Its motor revved through the street, then spluttered to a stop. Saira must have found someone to help me. I heard quick footsteps—those of two people. I looked across and saw the silhouettes of a man and a woman running towards the station. They stepped into the light. From one end to the other, we looked at each other, and we all gasped in astonishment synchronously. My wish had come true.

Chapter 10

Hope is Real

On the other side of the station stood my parents! My eyes filled with tears as I managed to say, "H-Hi!" I ran across the track and embraced them. "Anne!" my mother cried. My father hugged me tightly, holding back tears. Keller howled from the other end of the station, so I ran back to get her.

"This is my dog," I told them. "Keller." My father petted Keller between her ears while my mother gave a disgusted look. I giggled.

"I'm so sorry we lost you," my mother said, crying as she hugged me.

"We saw a picture of the last train to Pakistan from Bombay in the papers, and we found you," my father explained.

"We were in Rajasthan and took a train here as soon as we saw the picture. We stayed near the station until the train arrived. I'm sorry; I thought it would reach this morning."

I smiled. "No worries. I survived while you both were gone. I got attacked and faced danger, but I'm still here."

My parents hugged me, tears flowing. They kept apologising. "Don't worry," I reassured them. "We're together; that's all that matters."

"We need to get you home," my father said. "Let's take the ship back to Great Britain."

Before I knew it, we were on the ship back to Great Britain, in our little rooms, just like before. The horn blew as we sailed towards the horizon, leaving the coast of Pakistan behind. I waved goodbye to the country, to the changes I made, and to Saira. I hoped she lived a happy life, and India too. This trip taught me to consider both sides of a story and to see each perspective. I'm traveling home with my family with a moral lesson and a story to tell.

Story 2

In the Wake of Freedom: Mahesh's Quest

By Raphael Nair Lobo

The End of the Beginning

6:14 a.m., August 13, 1947

The dishes clanged that morning. The sky, tinged with orange, was filled with clouds. Akash Bhai, the bread vendor, was shouting for attention. Mahesh stepped onto the cold stone floor. "Mama?" Mahesh called out in a croaky voice. He walked into the kitchen and began to get ready for school. He saw his mother outside, hanging the clothes. Mahesh ran back into his room to get dressed, put on his uniform, and hurried out of the house.

4:30 p.m., August 13, 1947

Mahesh walked down the rough road, the heat slapping his face as he loosened his tie. Suddenly, he heard a loud noise. Two teenage boys were riding bicycles down the street. One of the boys was thrown off the dusty vehicle. "Get your Hindu faces off my road!" screamed a man in a white vest, his beard grimy and his forehead slick with sweat that reflected the ground. Mahesh watched as the boy, with a bloodied lip, jumped on the back of his friend's bike and rode away. Mahesh quickly fled the scene.

6:25 p.m., August 13, 1947

The sun rolled down the horizon, and the hot air began to stifle him. Sahiwal was a sweltering city, and the streets were eerily silent. Mahesh sat on his bed as his fan swirled around, shaking worryingly. He thought about the earlier incident and tossed restlessly on his bed. Suddenly, an Indie dog ran in. "Oh, Khushee," he said, his voice brightening. The dog jumped and wagged its tail. Mahesh walked out of his room, holding Khushee by the collar. He looked at his dog, and they both ran outside.

5:49 a.m., August 14, 1947

That morning felt different. The air was foggy. Mahesh walked to school for 30 minutes because large crowds were streaming across the muddy roads, throwing orange-petalled flowers. He thought nothing of it until a man in a white vest screamed, "India is free!" Mahesh's thoughts raced as he turned around in shock and quickly ran to school.

12:43 p.m., August 14, 1947

Mahesh's friend, Aqib, approached him with a sad expression. "India is split in two," he said, looking down.

"What do you mean by split?" Mahesh asked, confused.

"India is split into two parts. Mama told me."

They both sat down at their desks. Mahesh stared at his paper, troubled. As he pressed his pencil onto the page, he replayed the moment in his mind. "Split in half?" he thought, still writing English words over and over. When the bell rang, he rushed to Aqib.

"What do you mean?" Mahesh called out, holding back his emotions.

"Mahesh, there are now Pakistan and India. They are both independent countries now. And I will stay here in Pakistan," Aqib replied, walking out of the class.

Mahesh, feeling a surge of anxiety, darted to another classroom. Sahiwal is now part of Pakistan, not India.

7:45 p.m., August 14, 1947

Mahesh approached his grandmother. "Dadi, how come I didn't know about the partition?"

"Partition?" She shook her head, tsking. "Who told you this?"

"Aqib, Dadi."

"Don't listen to that boy. What lies he's telling?" Dadi replied.

But Mahesh could understand she was secretly lying. He then brought up the topic of independence, which briefly lifted Dadi's spirits before she became sombre again.

"The Brits are leaving, Dadi."

"I know, Mahesh," she replied in a monotone.

Mahesh realised that, out of all the houses in India, this one seemed the least excited about independence. At least, that was what he thought.

A Knock of Terror

12:32 a.m., August 15, 1947

That night, Mahesh barely slept for what felt like months. Screams and cheers erupted every minute. He finally got out of bed and looked through the small window. The commotion showed no sign of stopping. "Independence at last!" the people chanted happily. There was joy throughout the field. Little did they know that this happiness would soon turn to bloodshed.

11:47 a.m., August 20, 1947

A few days later, Mahesh woke to a loud knock and a cold screech. He recognised the sound as coming from Aisha Aunty, a neighbour two houses away. He quickly scrambled to his knees on the bed, peering out of the window. More screams filled the air as he rushed out of his room, terrified. "MAMA!!" he shouted, searching for his mother. He hadn't been this scared in years. Years ago, Mahesh's father had fallen to the floor, killed by a man from a neighbouring village. The man and Mahesh's father had had a violent argument over a complaint about a water incident involving Akash Bhai, the bread vendor. The man, a large, bearded figure around

45 years old, took the complaint seriously, and the conflict escalated over months. One Thursday, the man came to their town and stabbed Mahesh's father with a broken broom. Mahesh witnessed the entire incident. Years later, he was paralysed with fear. The screams continued to echo through the village until he heard a loud crash at the door.

Despair Beyond Compare

11:53 a.m., August 20, 1947

"Do not move," Dadi whispered, trembling. Mahesh was confused. Khushee was held between him and Dadi. Mama then ran in, her sari shimmering in the dim room. Suddenly, Akash Bhai burst in, panting. "Run! Didi! Bhago!" he cried, limping on one leg. The three of them hurried to the water tank, which stood about 65–80 feet tall. They hoped they were far from the riots. Mama helped Dadi up the metal stairs while Mahesh followed closely behind. As they climbed higher, Mama was suddenly overcome with guilt. "Oh God. We left Akshai Chacha at home. Mahesh, go get him now!" she screamed.

Mahesh quickly turned and ran back to the house. "Akshai Chacha?" he called, shaking his uncle awake. He helped him to the water tank, but as they approached, they were halted by the sound of a riot below. "Die, you Hindus!" the rioters shouted. Mahesh was stunned and wanted to confront them, but he reconsidered. The tower's strongest supporting pillar had been smashed into pieces by a rioter. The entire structure collapsed, accompanied by screams. Mahesh cried out, "MAMA, DADI, KHUSHEE!" A deafening crash echoed through the village. There was death and more death.

12:03 p.m., August 20, 1947

Mahesh searched for his family under the rubble for what felt like an eternity, but there was no hope. Blood stained the field. Chacha also searched as they hid from the rioters. Despair set in until they heard a faint squeal. It came from beneath a pile of large rocks. Mahesh and his uncle managed to pull out the source of the noise. "Khushee?" Mahesh whimpered, still in shock from the recent events. The dog responded with a soft whimper. Although slightly comforted, Mahesh was haunted by the earlier chaos. "Mahesh, we have to leave now," Chacha said, fear evident in his voice.

Adrift and Alone

2:31 p.m., August 20, 1947

Mahesh and his chacha fled the village with a few jugs of water and some rotis. They needed to catch a train that would take them to another train heading to the border. Since they were Hindus, they were heading to India. The journey to the train station was a 30-minute walk or a 20-minute run, and they had to make it on time.

3:04 p.m., August 20, 1947

On the train, families were packed everywhere, even on the roof. The chaos was overwhelming. Suddenly, a Hindu man burst into their car from another train and shouted, "Retreat! RETREAT!" Families scrambled to their feet, creating a cacophony of movement. Chacha was about to rise when a Muslim soldier entered the car, holding a shotgun. Mahesh, seeing the soldier, grabbed Khushee and called out for his chacha. He spotted him moving through the crowd towards him. But then, BANG! BANG!! BANG!!! Three shots rang out, and Akshai Chacha's knees gave way, collapsing to the floor. "CHACHA!!!" Mahesh screamed, desperately searching through the panicked crowd. The only people who truly mattered to him were gone. Khushee whimpered, sensing the gravity of the situation. Mahesh had to find a place to stay on the train. It was another hour to the next station, according to what he had heard. But he had no idea where to go once he reached India. He needed his uncle. He needed his family. But for now, it was just an 11-year-old boy and his dog, stranded and lost amid the chaos of a killing spree.

Help from Unknown Places

5:12 p.m., August 20, 1947

Today was overwhelming. Mahesh sat on the grimy blue floor of the train with Khushee, tears streaming down his face. He was lost and didn't know what to do. "What's outside Sahiwal?" he wondered. The boy had never been beyond the city. He remembered having relatives in India. "RELATIVES!" he suddenly realised. But where in India were they? He recalled Papa mentioning family members there years ago before he died. He had said they were in Chapur. No, wait, Chatpur? He wasn't sure of the exact name, but it was close. However, it would take 5–6 hours to reach the border. They had already been travelling for two hours. The journey seemed even longer with the weight of his losses.

9:23 p.m., August 20, 1947

The train wheels screeched and sparked as it came to a stop. People scrambled through the compartments, searching for their loved ones. Mahesh awoke from a 4-hour nap, exhausted but determined. He walked out with Khushee amidst the chaos, where people jostled and shouted. Some remained silent, while others screamed and argued. He was getting closer; it was only a little further to the border. And then Cha, Chat, Chatpur? He recalled struggling with the name. Suddenly, a man appeared on the station platform. He looked homeless, like many others. He noticed Mahesh's confusion and approached him. "What's wrong, beta?" the man asked. Mahesh explained his struggle with the name.

"Chhatarpur," the man said. "It's named after King Chhatarsal, who never lost a war. His bravery should inspire you to reach your destination and stay safe. In that way, you, too, will overcome this battle." The man's words offered Mahesh a glimmer of hope.

Lost and Found

5:34 a.m., August 21, 1947

Mahesh woke up, resting against a wall. As he looked around, he realised he was beside the tracks. He rubbed his eyes, thinking it must be a dream. The loud blast of a train horn jolted him awake. He quickly looked left and right before crossing the tracks to the other side, which was the correct route to the border. But as he walked down the tracks, he suddenly remembered... He had forgotten Khashee! Mahesh froze in fear. Just as he was about to turn around, he heard another loud horn. His heart raced wildly, and he saw his life flash before his eyes. At that moment, something jumped off the platform and onto the tracks, pushing Mahesh into the air and onto the opposite side. He felt a soft, furry presence against him. It was his dog. "KHUSHEE!!!!!" He cried out in anguish. He glanced back, thinking he had heard one final squeal as the train dragged the dog down the track. The train stopped. Mahesh scrambled to get under the train as quickly as he could and saw Khushee lying on the ground.

Relief washed over him when he discovered the dog was alive. "Khushee?" Mahesh asked as he pulled her onto the platform. Despite being small enough to survive, Khushee had sustained some bruises. The two of them ran out of the station and continued their journey. Mahesh was grateful to still have some water and roti that kind people had given him out of pity. They had a walk to the next station, followed by a 4-hour journey to Chhatarpur. Mahesh hoped his relatives would recognise him and take care of him, and most importantly, that they were still there. He also needed to know where they lived in Chhatarpur. For now, he just needed to make it there.

8:32 a.m., August 21, 1947

Mahesh arrived at the train station with the help of the old man. "I never asked, but what's your name?" Mahesh inquired.

"Mahendra. But call me anything you want," replied the old man.

"My name is Mahesh," Mahesh said.

They had gotten along well, but they had to part ways soon. Mahesh had been waiting for the train for a while when he noticed a sign for Khanna Hospital outside the station. Feeling exhausted, he decided to take a short walk there to see if they could check on Khushee's bruises. Inside the hospital, he saw that it was filled with injured and dying people. He felt a deep sadness for them but was startled when he bumped into a man being assisted by a nurse. A familiar scent reached him. He realised he was standing right in front of Chacha. "CHA…CHA!!!" he exclaimed with hope. Khushee wagged her tail as fast as a plane's propeller. Mahesh's Chacha was equally overjoyed. They were reunited, and the three of them left the hospital in happiness. It was time to catch the train.

A Knock of Hope

12:43 p.m., August 21, 1947

The horn blared at every station. People were lying down on the floor and everywhere. Mahesh had no choice but to sit on top of the train with his dog and uncle. Mahesh had never sat on top of a train before. He climbed up from the side of a window. It was scary at first, but he soon got used to it. Many people were up there as well. The train started moving, shaking initially. The speed built up to about 40 mph. Everything was going well until a man got up and ran towards them. He told them to get off the train and then screamed, "GET OFF THE TRAIN, MUSLIMS!!!!" Chacha explained that they were Hindus, not Muslims, but the man disagreed. "What's that on your head then!?" Chacha had been wearing a topi-like hat to hide from the Muslims fighting in Sahiwal and had kept it on until now. The man screamed at him and then grabbed Mahesh by the hand, threatening to kill him. Chacha stood up and pleaded for the man to put Mahesh down. The man complied, but not in the way Chacha intended. Mahesh was thrown off the train and fell onto the yellow grass below. He felt pain in his bones upon impact. Chacha then jumped off in a controlled manner, grabbed Mahesh, and managed to climb back up as the train slowed down. Mahesh felt a sharp pain in his hand but was otherwise alright.

5:23 a.m., August 22, 1947

A day had passed on the train, and Khushee was drenched from the monsoon rains. So were the other two. It would be another day before they reached their destination. Chacha climbed back into the compartment and saw a man selling drinks from a hot flask of chai. Chacha paid for it and brought a cup for Mahesh, as well as some hot water for Khushee. The chai was refreshing to Mahesh since he hadn't had much to drink in a long time. The three of them sat on top of the train as the breeze flowed through their hair. It was a beautiful day, and the view from up there was amazing. Mahesh thought about how lucky he was to have survived the recent events. "Maybe Chhatarpur is a good place. Maybe it's where I belong," he thought as he gazed at the blue and grey sky.

3:45 p.m., August 23, 1947

Mahesh felt the air, and it seemed unfamiliar. Chacha told him they were close now. Soon, Mahesh saw the greenest land he had seen in what felt like a very long time. It lifted his spirits as the train horn blasted. Mahesh had found a home. Chacha, Khushee, and Mahesh all exclaimed (with Khushee barking), "We're HOME!! Or are we?" It had been a long, hard journey for Mahesh. Chacha got them some daal baati, which they enjoyed but ate in silence. The place looked spectacular. They then explored the station. It was time to find their relatives. They walked the streets for a while, searching for the house, but deep down, they were worried about whether the relatives would remember them and accept them. Chacha had only met the grandmother, who was about 95 years old. They had gotten along very well when he was a child. Now, she was their only hope.

6:13 p.m., August 23, 1947

They arrived at the door. Mahesh looked at Chacha nervously, holding Khushee in his arms. He kept pacing, thinking about what to say. Then Chacha took a deep breath and raised his hand to knock on the door. The door creaked open as an eye peeped through the crevice.

"Kaun hai?" the eye inquired.

"Dadima hai?" Chacha asked. "Mein Akshai, Sahiwal se aaya hoon," he said.

Inside, a loud voice exclaimed, "Akshai! Mera bachha!" The eye, which belonged to a boy about Mahesh's age, opened the door.

"Dadima!!!" Chacha ran towards his grandmother and hugged her. At that moment, Mahesh knew he was home.